About the Author

Semi-retired, and wondering how to entertain the grandchildren during the pandemic lockdown, I can think of nothing better to do than to continue to write a story for my grandchildren to read which I started to write for my daughter, Cari. They enjoyed reading it and I hope you do too.

THE WOLF GODS

STUART HANCOX

THE WOLF GODS

Nightingale Books

NIGHTINGALE PAPERBACK

© Copyright 2022
Stuart Hancox

The right of Stuart Hancox to be identified as author of
this work has been asserted by him in accordance with the
Copyright, Designs and Patents Act 1988.

All Rights Reserved

No reproduction, copy or transmission of this publication
may be made without written permission.
No paragraph of this publication may be reproduced,
copied or transmitted save with the written permission of the
publisher, or in accordance with the provisions
of the Copyright Act 1956 (as amended).

Any person who commits any unauthorised act in relation to
this publication may be liable to criminal
prosecution and civil claims for damages.

A CIP catalogue record for this title is
available from the British Library.
ISBN 978 1 83875 276 7

*Nightingale Books is an imprint of
Pegasus Elliot MacKenzie Publishers Ltd.*
www.pegasuspublishers.com

First Published in 2022

**Nightingale Books
Sheraton House Castle Park
Cambridge England**

Printed & Bound in Great Britain

Dedication

I dedicate this book in remembrance of our pet
Samoyed, Sam, and to my daughter and grandchildren,
fantasy being a necessary ingredient for living.

END OF TERM

It was a hot summer's day, with a warm gentle breeze. This was the day that Cari had been counting down to, it was the last school day, the end of the school term and the start of the summer holidays. Cari ran from the classroom to greet her mum who was waiting for her in the school playground.

"No more school for six weeks, *yippeee!*"

Cari's mum was thinking, probably like every other parent at that moment, six weeks of what to do!

The walk from school was full of talking about what was for dinner that night, and where were they going on holiday once Dad had finished work.

"Chicken nuggets and chips tonight because Dad is working late," said Mum.

They arrived home and Cari's mum started to prepare the evening meal.

"I'm going to lie down outside," said Cari. "Call me when it's ready."

Cari spread an old play carpet on the patio and lay down. She closed her eyes, she could feel the heat of the sun beating down. There was a gentle warm breeze now and then, and she could hear her mum working in the kitchen, preparing the evening meal.

Cari had a dog called Sam. He was a Samoyed, a sleigh dog, and he had pure white fur with a mane around his neck similar to a lion.

Sam was a very large and powerful animal, but was very gentle; he always stood proud and had the look that gave Cari reassurance that he would always be around to protect his family if he needed to, and always ensure that his family safety would be his main priority.

Cari lay on the carpet still wondering where they would be going on holiday. Dad had been planning something but never said where they were going.

There were light fluffy clouds spaced out in the sky, and every now and then one would pass in front of the sun casting a shadow on the patio, blocking out the sun for just a few seconds.

When this happened, Cari opened her eyes and could see her mum at the kitchen window washing dishes in the sink. "Is tea ready yet?" shouted Cari.

"Not yet," replied her mum. "I'll call you when it's ready."

Cari closed her eyes again and felt the sun once more as it showed itself from behind the cloud which had covered it.

She could still hear her mum working in the kitchen and feel the warm breeze and the heat of the sun. It was very relaxing, and even more so knowing that she had no school or homework to do for a whole six weeks.

Another shadow covered her as she lay with her eyes closed and she waited for it to pass to feel the sun once again on her face.

This shadow is taking longer to pass, she thought, and opened her eyes to see Sam standing over her. "Move, Sam, you're blocking the sun," Cari said, as she tried to push him away.

But Sam was very large and very difficult to move, if he didn't want to be moved.

THE JOURNEY

"Sam will you get out of the way."

Sam stood over Cari and gave a deep slow growl.

Cari called to her mum, "Mum, tell Sam to get out of the way, he's standing over me blocking the sun." There was no reply from her mum and Cari thought that her mum must have left the kitchen, because she couldn't hear her working there any more.

"Oh! Shift, Sam." Cari tried pushing harder on Sam's neck to move him but he wasn't going anywhere.

Sam looked up and sniffed the air; he gave another long deep growl.

Cari looked towards the kitchen window and could still see her mum standing there. "Mum, tell Sam to move," she shouted.

Cari stared at the kitchen window with her mum clearly standing there, she was looking out onto the patio area where Cari was lying.

She wasn't moving and Cari noticed that there was no sound as she had heard before; there was a stillness and quietness in the air that was quite unnerving.

Sam lowered his head and looked into Cari's eyes, and then what should have been frightening to say the least, but knowing Sam would never harm his family, and also knowing that he had a very kind, and trustworthy nature, he did the most unexpected thing you would ever believe possible. He spoke, "Hold on tight," he said, in a calm, deep voice. His voice was husky, and it sounded as though he had a sore throat, but I suppose that is what you would have expected from a Samoyed breed sleigh dog.

"Hold on very tight to my mane," said Sam.

Cari trusted Sam, and even though she should have been alarmed at hearing him talk, felt very calm, as though it was nothing unusual.

There was a strange crackling sound, the ground started to tremble, and a mist appeared from nowhere, making it very difficult for Cari to see anything other than her much loved pet dog, Sam.

"What's happening?" Cari asked, in a shaky voice not knowing if anyone would even hear her, or reply.

Sam spoke again. "I will explain when we have completed our journey. For now, just hold tight and everything will be okay."

"Why, where are we going, what's happening?" Cari asked once more.

Sam replied, "I will explain soon, just hold on tight."

Sam raised his head and gave out a piercing howl like Cari had never heard before. It echoed all around and the crackling sounds got louder, and the mist thicker. The once gentle breeze turned into a strong gust of wind.

Cari just closed her eyes and did what Sam said — she held on very tight to the mane around his neck.

Then, all of a sudden, it all went quiet and still. Cari opened her eyes and saw Sam looking at her.

"We have arrived," said Sam.

"Arrived where, what do you mean?" asked Cari.

"We are safe now, you can let go of my mane and I will try to explain," said Sam.

THE WOLF GOD ZEFF (SAM)

Cari let go of Sam's mane and Sam stepped away from her. Cari sat up, and looked all around her. "Where are we? Where's the house gone?"

Sam sat beside Cari and started to explain who he was, and what had happened.

"To you, I am Sam, your pet and protector, but I am much more than that. I am, in spirit, a direct descendant from the wolf gods. I am son of Lupa and Conri. My name is Zeff, the wolf god of strength, power and stability of mountains, rocks, sand and earth. The spirit of dominance,"

"I don't understand," said Cari, "you are Sam, but you can talk, and we are somewhere away from home, I can't see my house anywhere."

"Don't be alarmed," said Sam. "I appear to you as a Samoyed dog," he continued. "So as not to frighten you or the family that I choose to live with, and protect."

Sam stood up and sniffed the air, then continued to explain. "My wolf spirit passes down through generations, and up until this moment in time, I have had no need to identify myself to you."

"So, where are we?" asked Cari.

Sam walked around still sniffing the air and continued to explain where they were, and what had just happened.

"We are still at home, but in between time. Something has happened to make time as you know it unstable, and crack open. We have passed through a crack in time, that's what the noise was you were hearing, it was the window in time cracking open."

Sam stopped sniffing the air and looked towards a hill that stood in the distance. There were trees scattered all around, not close together but spaced out, they looked like they were standing in lines. You could see the way ahead as though the trees were giving direction to travel in.

"We need to go to the hill, to find the curator, the guardian of the window in time."

Cari and Sam started to walk towards the hill in the distance.

"Well," said Cari, "at least it's still a nice day here, wherever we are."

Cari thought to herself that even though there were no buildings around, the layout of the land still looked familiar, like the hill they were walking towards looked very much like the hill near her home that had a ruined castle on it.

"Why am I here with you?" asked Cari.

Sam stopped walking and looked deep in thought for a few seconds before answering. "It seems to me that the curator has a problem that requires me to have an assistant." Sam continued to walk. "Come on, Cari, try to keep up."

They walked through fields lined with trees. There didn't seem to be any signs of a road or path to follow, but then Cari did notice that the trees did form a line of sorts, creating what could be assumed as being a path to follow. "What do we do when we get to the hill" Cari asked.

"I know as much as you at the moment," Sam replied. "All I know is, we need to go to the hill, my nose is pulling me that way."

They walked for what seemed to Cari to be a very long way, and the hill didn't seem to be getting that much closer.

Cari was starting to get a little bit tired of walking. "Maybe your nose is pulling you towards a bone or pig's ear to eat," she said in a grumpy tone.

Sam just ignored what Cari said. He knew she was getting tired, after all she'd not long just finished a full day in school and was probably feeling hungry too.

"We will stop and rest for a while in the shade of that tree; it will give me time to think too."

They stopped walking and Cari sat under the shade of a tree, and Sam lay down next to her.

They both looked towards the hill which was plain to see following the line of the trees, Sam was sure they needed to go there. Suddenly he stood up, glaring ahead with ears pricked up.

"What is it, Sam?" asked Cari.

"I'm sure I saw something in the distance coming this way," replied Sam. "Well, it seems we will soon have company."

Cari stood up and looked in the same direction as Sam "I can't see anything."

"My vision is far superior to yours," said Sam, "and, yes, we will have company very soon, and I can now see who it is," said Sam.

"Who is it then?" asked Cari.

Sam looked at Cari and said, "It's someone I have not seen for a very long time." Sam raised his head and gave out a very loud howl.

Then, a few seconds later, a returning howl was heard.

"Who is it, Sam?" asked Cari.

"It's one of my brothers," said Sam.

"You have brothers like yourself?" asked Cari.

"Yes," said Sam. "I have two brothers, Marrok, Amoux, and a sister, Amarok."

"Which one is it then?" asked Cari in a shaky voice.

Sam heard the fear in her voice, a strange wolf dog that she didn't know was soon to be with them. "There is no need to be afraid," said Sam. "We are all of the same family and serve the same course."

The visitor got closer, and Sam could finally see which brother it was who would soon be joining them.

"It's Amoux," Sam looked very happy to see his brother.

"So what kind of wolf god is he?" Cari asked.

"Amoux is the wolf god of birds bats, sky, wind, weather and flight. He is the spirit of freedom."

"That's just great," said Cari. "Birds and bats; you know I don't like them."

THE WOLF GOD AMOUX (MAX)

"Don't worry yourself, he can control them, and they do his bidding, without question," said Sam.

Amoux arrived slightly out of breath and Sam greeted him with excitement, having not seen him for a very long time.

When Sam and Amoux had calmed down from their excitement of reuniting with each other, Amoux looked at Cari and said, "This is a human, what, how, why have you brought a human here, Zeff?"

Sam told Amoux that he had no choice. "This is Cari, my master, we were both in our home when time cracked open. We were both pulled here together. Have you seen the Curator?"

Amoux replied, shaking his head and walking around looking agitated. "This is not a place for a human to be. The curator is waiting to see us both together, it wouldn't see me alone."

"Is our other brother here, too?" asked Sam.

"No," said Amoux. "I was told by the birds that I'd find you here. It looks like curator has only summoned you and me."

Amoux walked over to Cari to introduce himself. "I am sorry if I alarmed you, this was not my intention.

You can call me Max, that's what my master calls me. By what name do you call my brother, Zeff?"

"I named him, Sam," replied Cari.

"Are you rested enough?" asked Sam, looking at Cari.

"Yes, I think so," said Cari.

"Then we should be on our way to find out what this is all about."

They all started a slow walk towards the hill that lay ahead.

"Sam?" asked Cari. "You said you are brothers, but why does Max look so very different than you?"

"Well," said Sam, "we are brothers in spirit form, not in bodily form. To humans I look like a sleigh dog, the breed of a Samoyed, as does Marrok. Max looks like what humans call German a Shepherd."

"And what about your sister, Amarock?" asked Cari. "What does she look like?"

Sam was a bit hesitant to reply, but knew he had to. "Amarock is so very different from us. She is so very fierce and frightening, everyone is so scared of her and that's why she prefers her own company. She appears to humans as a Rottweiler, a devil dog."

Cari could hear birds singing, and pushed her way to walk between Sam and Max. This made her feel slightly more comfortable, especially as Sam had told her that Max could control the birds.

Sam and Max walked at a pace that was comfortable for Cari.

"So, is this curator an animal too?" asked Cari.

Sam and Max looked at each other and grinned.

Sam replied, "The curator is something and nothing. It exists but doesn't exist, it lives between time and keeps time in time, with time at the time it should be in."

Cari didn't understand and was confused with what Sam was trying to explain, but looked at him and just said, "Oh."

Cari could still hear birds singing but had never looked up in the trees until now. The trees where full of birds, and as they passed each tree, the birds sitting on the branches would sing out. They all seemed to bow their heads as if to honour Max passing amongst them.

Cari asked Sam and Max, "What are the powers of your other brother and sister then?"

"Well," said Sam, "Amarok mainly appears at night. She is the spirit of the forest, and god of regret. She is a night hunter of loneliness. She only ever liked her own company, not a wolf you would like to meet if you were travelling alone, especially at night. She has always been different and I don't even think she has ever lived with a human family."

Max continued, "Marrok controls seas and rivers. He has control of water and everything living in it. He is also the spirit of memory. It would be comforting if he were to join us too."

Sam agreed with Max on this, "I would like to know why he isn't here with us, too," said Sam.

"The curator must have his reasons," replied Max.

Cari thought to herself, Max seems very nice, but it doesn't sound like the sister, Amarok, would be a very friendly wolf to meet.

They eventually arrived at the foot of the hill.

"Do you know where we go now?" asked Sam, looking at Max.

"I think we just have to wait until the curator is ready for us," replied Max.

They all sat together at the foot of the hill waiting for a sign of what to do or where to go next.

Suddenly clouds started to appear in a very strange formation. "What is that Max?" asked Sam.

"Nothing to do with me," replied Max. "I haven't summoned any change in the weather."

Then the ground started to shake. "An earthquake," said Cari.

"Well, that's nothing to do with me," said Sam. Sam tried to stop the earth from shaking using his powers, he gave a very long and deep growl, but his powers seemed to have no control over the quake.

"You losing control?" asked Max looking at Sam.

"No more than you," replied Sam.

The earth fell away from the side of the hill to reveal a shallow cave. "Looks like we've got some shelter, anyway, if it starts to rain," said Cari.

She had no sooner finished her statement when the clouds burst, and rain fell like a waterfall filling the hollowed ground in front of them caused by the earthquake.

They all ran for cover in the cave, looking at the rain fall.

"That's strange," said Max. "It's only raining over the hollow ground between the trees."

The hollowed-out ground very quickly filled with water forming a large pond.

The ground quaked again and the water from the pond seemed to rise, like a curtain back up into the clouds, leaving small puddles and a thick fog like mist behind.

Sam and Max looked at each other and then stared into the mist.

"Do you see something?" asked Max.

"I most certainly do," replied Sam.

Sam turned to Cari. "He always was a bit of a performer."

"Who was?" asked Cari.

"Marrok," replied Sam. "Marrok is here."

"Hey, Marrok," shouted Max, "over here."

Marrok turned and looked toward them all standing in their shelter, looking all around as he approached them. "What's going on?"

THE CAVE ON THE HILLSIDE
THE WOLF GOD MARROK (FLUFF)

"I was just taking a swim in the river when the water dragged me down, and I ended up here. Still, it's nice to see my brothers again after so long being apart."

Sam introduced Cari to Marrok. "This is Cari, my master," Sam continued. "It seems that we were all summoned here for a reason by the curator"

Sam told Marrok that to make names easier for Cari to remember, they were using their given names, names given to them by their masters.

"Cari has named me Sam," said Zeff. "Amoux's master named him Max, so what can Cari call you?"

Marrok looked stunned, or maybe it was just hesitance of revealing his given name.

"Well," said Sam, "what is your given name?"

Marrok replied in a very low soft voice, "Fluff."

"What was that?" asked Sam

"Okay, it's *Fluff*," blurted out Marrok.

Cari thought that was a nice name because Samoyeds are very fluffy.

Max just rolled around on the floor laughing uncontrollably.

"Come on now," said Sam, "it's a name given by a human. It's just something Marrok has to live with for a short time"

"But *Fluff*," blurted out Max, in fits of laughter.

Marrok turned away, and Cari went over to comfort him. "I think it's a very nice name," said Cari.

"Take control of yourself, Max," said Sam. "It's a human that named him. It's not going to be with him for eternity."

"Have you forgotten the time that you were named Bubbles by your human master when you were in the form of a poodle?"

That seemed to bring back memories. Max coughed and composed himself.

Sam looked at his brothers and Cari. "Well, I can't see the curator summoning Amarok to be with us, he never has in the past. So I must assume we are now complete, and waiting to be seen."

Cari said, "You mean you have done this before?"

"We have been summoned together in different parts of this earth's history by the curator, but we can never remember why or what for, we only remember being together and in the presence of the curator," said Sam.

They were all looking out of the shelter. The clouds had disappeared, and the pond had almost completely dried up. Birds were drinking and bathing in the shallow puddles left behind.

Something made Cari turn to look behind her. "Look, a door, that wasn't there before."

They all turned and looked at the door then at each other.

"Well," said Cari, "who's going to knock?"

"I'll do it," said Max. He raised his head and gave out a soft gentle woof, to which, a woodpecker acknowledged him, flew past them all and started pecking on the door like a door knocker. Cari was startled and jumped to grab Sam's fur around his neck; this gave her some reassurance and comfort.

Sam explained to Max and Fluff that Cari had a fear of birds.

"I'm sorry," said Max. "I do understand how you feel, everyone has a fear of something."

The door opened, and the bird was dismissed by Max, but looked very pleased that he had been of service to his master.

Beyond the door was a passageway lit up by fire torches, hanging from the stone lined walls.

The passageway was wide enough for them to walk two abreast, but Sam took the lead, followed by Cari. Max and Fluff walked side by side, chatting to each other in dog language.

"Let's see what awaits us," said Sam.

THE QUEST

They all followed Sam along the passage, which seemed to be going into the centre of the hill.

Cari couldn't help but notice how the walls of the passage looked. The walls were covered in so many different coloured mosses like she had never seen before, and as the light from the torches lit up their way, sparkling stones embedded in the walls glistened and sparkled, like different coloured diamonds.

The passage eventually opened up into a large cavern. There was a table in the centre of the cavern laid out with food, a bright light shining down onto it from above.

They all moved towards the table, then a soft voice spoke.

"Welcome, Zeff, Cari, Amoux and Marrok, please be seated and eat, I will join with you shortly."

They all sat around the table. Cari and her companions helped themselves to the variety of food laid out upon it.

They all finished eating and waited for the arrival of the curator.

The room was very quiet. Nobody moved, then, a faint sound of footsteps could be heard approaching.

As the sound of footsteps got closer, the light shining from above onto the table dimmed. A multi-coloured glow started to show itself from another passage that had appeared without anyone noticing it being there before.

The glow didn't seem to have any physical form, but footsteps were moving with it.

Sam, being the dominant leader, stood up as the footsteps stopped, and looked towards the glow. "My senses tell me you are the curator, but you have no physical form. What has happened?"

The curator spoke, and as it did so, the glow changed colours, giving the appearance of a slow-moving light show.

"I have summoned you here to help me. I am having trouble keeping time in balance, as you have noticed. I cannot do this alone, because I have no physical form. I am using all my powers to try to keep time as stable as I can. That is why you only see me this way."

Sam spoke, "What has caused this to happen?"

"I was visited by the wolf god, Anubis. He did not show his true recognisable form. I have no idea how he arrived here, but he appeared to me as a travelling beggar, in need of help. I gave him food and shelter, a place for him to rest, and I was repaid by him stealing the wolf head from the top of my staff, which I would like Cari to take hold of."

A wooden staff floated through the air and landed on the table in front of Cari. The staff was like a long walking stick with a cup shaped top.

Sam, Max, Fluff and Cari stared at the stick lying on the table. Cari turned to Sam and asked, "Who is this Anubis then?"

Sam looked at each of his brothers before replying. "Anubis is not of this world, but is of this time. He is a half-breed — part human, part wolf — the god of bad and evil things, the god of the dead."

"That's scary, and what about the wolf head missing from this staff?" asked Cari

"The wolf head is the source of power that keeps his place of the dead in its own time. It keeps his world apart and sealed, stopping it from merging with the time of the living," explained the curator. "If it remains with him, he will crack open time completely and all evil will roam freely under his control."

"How much time can you give us?" asked Sam, looking at the curator's energy glow.

"I will keep time here stable her for as long as I can," replied the curator. "You should go now. He will be heading for the sacrificial stone of Tizoc, which stands at the top of this hill. There he will offer the wolf head to his own staff, and place it on the stone of Tizoc. If he manages to do this then we would have failed and time as Cari knows it will not exist any more."

They all stood up from sitting around the table and looked at each other.

Cari looked at the staff and picked it up, then they all started to walk back along the passage to the opening of the cave.

"This is not good at all," said Sam. "I can already feel instability growing and gaining strength."

Max and Fluff agreed they could feel changes too with the head missing from the curator's staff.

They walked back along the moss lined passage to the door that they had entered through. They walked outside, turned and looked up at the hill in front of them.

"We will need to use every power we have if we are going to succeed in this," Sam said. "At least Anubis won't know, or shouldn't know, we are here on his trail chasing him."

They all started to climb the hill. It was very steep and Cari, only having two legs, found it very difficult.

"Wait a minute," said Sam. "I can make things a little easier."

Sam raised his head and gave out a soft grrrufff with that, earth started to move in front of them, and slowly, a winding path appeared in the hillside.

"This should make the journey slightly easier," said Sam.

They continued along the winding path heading to the top of the hill.

Even though Sam had made a path for them to follow, and make the climb a little easier, it was still tiring in the heat of the day, and made them all very thirsty.

"I'm thirsty," said Cari.

"I think we could all do with a drink, and rest," said Fluff.

They found a nice shaded area by a wall of rocks, with short grass that looked like it had been freshly cut, and they all sat down to rest.

Fluff scratched at the rocks and a trickle of water appeared. He scratched once more, and the flow became stronger, turning into a small waterfall. "We can all drink, now," he said.

Sam, Max and Fluff lapped the flowing water up with their tongues, while Cari collected some water in the cup shape at the top of the staff she was carrying.

The water was very cool and refreshing.

"Mmmm that tastes so nice, apple flavour," said Cari, taking another sip from the cup.

Fluff laughed. "I forgot to tell you it would taste like anything you would like it to."

"Good job I was only thinking of cool water then," said Sam.

When they had refreshed themselves, Fluff tapped on the opening to the flow of water and it sealed itself.

"Don't want to wash the hill away, do we," Fluff said as the trickle slowly stopped.

"Come on then," said Sam. "We have no time to waste, do we?"

Time was something that didn't really exist as Cari knew it where they were, but with the curator still in control, Cari hoped all things would soon be back to the normality that she was used to.

They continued their journey and Sam couldn't help but notice that the path he had created was starting to change, it was decaying, falling apart.

"He seems to be gaining strength as he approaches the summit with the head of the staff," Sam said, as he looked at the crumbling pathway.

Cracks were emerging, making it more difficult to walk; they had to be careful where they were stepping. Cari used the staff as a walking stick to help steady herself, but tripped and stumbled a few times, managing to grab hold of Sam to stop herself from falling back down the hill.

Not only that, shadows seemed to be rising from the cracks that were opening in the pathway.

"Can you see them?" asked Cari. "Those shadowy things, what are they?"

"Yes, we can," replied Sam, Max and Fluff all together.

"Those are evil spirits, followers of Anubis from the underworld," continued Sam.

The shadowy shapes gathered in groups and charged towards Cari and her companions.

Although the shapes were only shadows and had no mass, they were still disturbing and frightened Cari.

"That's enough," said Max. "I'll put an end to this." Max looked up to the sky and made a noise, "Wowowowowowowow."

With that, a sudden strong gust of wind came and gathered the shadows together, the wind, doing the bidding of Max, had collected the shadows and was carrying them away.

Sam tried his best to repair the pathway, but found it increasingly difficult as they got closer and closer to the summit.

"We need eyes in the sky," said Max. "I will summon a bird of prey to view the hill from above."

Cari, on hearing the word bird, started to look all around feeling extremely nervous.

Max noticed this. "no need to worry yourself, Cari, I told you I do understand how you feel about birds, Sam told me, you will not see or hear it. The bird will fly very high, so that Anubis will not suspect he is being spied upon."

Anubis being half human and half wolf, and only having two legs, was not too far ahead and getting very close to the summit. He could now see the stone of Tizoc and felt that very soon he would have complete control of the living, as well as the dead.

Anubis was feeling very sure that nothing could stop him now from reaching the stone of Tizoc, and placing the wolf head on his staff.

The bird of prey which was summoned by Max circled high above Anubis, and Max could see through the eyes of the bird.

"He is very close to the stone of Tizoc," said Max. "We need to slow him down."

Sam turned to Cari. "You must now be very brave. We need to run ahead and do our best to stop him getting to the Tizoc stone."

"You mean you are leaving me on my own?" Cari said in a shaky voice. She was now very frightened.

She would be alone on a hill, in a strange place, and felt she would have no protection from anything.

"I will keep you protected from any harm," said Max. "The birds that you fear will keep their distance but keep watch over you."

Cari didn't really feel any comfort from that, after all how could a bird help in any way?

Cari continued walking on her own constantly looking all around, while Sam, Max and Fluff ran ahead to confront Anubis.

The pathway was getting more and more difficult for Cari to walk along. I wish Sam was here with me, Cari thought to herself.

Now and then she thought she could hear noises, like her mum still working in the kitchen.

She tried shouting, *"Mum, are you there?"*

There was no reply, how could she be here, thought Cari, this isn't a real place. Maybe, I'm asleep and dreaming, and Mum will wake me up when dinner is ready. But if I'm dreaming, why can't I wake up? Everything looks, feels, and smells so real.

Cari's thoughts were interrupted by more cracks appearing in the ground ahead of her.

I need to move faster, she thought to herself. I need to catch up with Sam, Max and Fluff, I feel safer with them.

She looked up to the sky and even though she was frightened of birds, she thought if she caught a glimpse of the eagle watching over her, she would feel reassured, that she would be safe from harm.

From her position on the hillside Cari could see the sun starting to set on the horizon. It would be getting dark soon, and she wouldn't be able to see where she was walking, this frightened her.

The hilltop still seemed so far away. I do wish Sam, Max and Fluff were here, she thought to herself. Cari tried to stay focused on the path and not letting her imagination take control.

"I am not afraid, I am not afraid, I am not afraid." She kept repeating this over and over again, trying to convince herself that she actually wasn't afraid, when really, she was.

Sam, Max and Fluff were approaching the top of the hill. They could see Anubis ahead of them getting closer to the stone of Tizoc.

"We need to split up and confront him from different directions. We need to slow him down using our powers," said Sam.

ANUBIS, GOD OF THE DEAD
THE CONFRONTATION

Sam, Max, and Fluff parted from each other. Sam stayed in the centre position, while Max moved away to Sam's left, and Fluff moved away to Sam's right.

They were now at equal distance from each other and Anubis.

Anubis was getting closer to his goal, and Sam was getting anxious to attack, but knew if he did, then all might be lost.

Sam pounded the ground with his paws, and upon each pounding the ground shook beneath Anubis's feet, making him unsteady.

Anubis turned around and saw Sam. "You are here. I was wondering if you would turn up. Does the curator think you alone will be able to stop me?" Anubis was struggling to stay upright on his two legs. The ground was shaking so violently with each pounding of Sam's paws beating upon it.

Anubis held the head of the curator's staff in his left hand, and his staff in his right.

"Look, Zeff," shouted Anubis, holding the wolf head above his head. "I will soon have the power of the curator in my hands, and you will do my bidding."

Max had not been noticed by Anubis, and summoned the eagle circling above to swoop down. The eagle knocked the wolf head from Anubis's hand.

Anubis turned to his right and saw Max. "So, Amoux, now there are two of you." Anubis, still struggling to stay upright, waved his staff in the air, then thrust it into the ground. The ground cracked open and his followers with shape but no solid form as yet, emerged, and charged at Sam and Max, trying to distract them.

"And do you think I would let my brothers have all the fun?" shouted Fluff.

Anubis turned to his left. "So, you too, Marrok, think you can stop me now? Even with your powers combined, do you think you can stop me now that I am this close to the Tizoc Stone?"

With the ground still trembling from Sam's pounding, the head of the staff had rolled part way down the hill and Anubis had dropped to his knees and started to crawl after it.

Fluff howled, and to no surprise the wind howled back with such force as to slow Anubis's progress on reaching the wolf head, which he needed to be placed on his own staff to gain control.

DARKNESS FALLS

Cari was starting to have difficulty in seeing the path, and the cracks that were increasing in number, and size.

She was getting very afraid, being alone in this strange place and not knowing where Sam was, or what Sam was doing.

I wish I had some company, she thought to herself.

She prodded the ground with the staff the curator had given her before each step, to make sure the ground was still firm beneath her feet. "I'll never get to the top of this hill," she said out loud.

"Maybe you won't," came a reply in a slow menacing voice.

"Who is that?" shouted Cari. "Who's there?"

Cari stared very hard, looking into the darkness, and saw two red eyes glaring at her.

"Who are you, what are you?" Cari's voice was trembling with fear.

"Does it really matter who or what I am?" came the reply.

"Show yourself," Cari held the staff in front of herself with both hands, ready to attack whatever, or whoever, it was that was answering her.

A shape slowly emerged from the darkness; it was a wolf with piercing, burning eyes.

"Stay away," shouted Cari. "I have friends here with me, you'd better stay away."

"I only see you, a lonely traveller," the reply came in a menacing tone.

The wolf slowly moved towards Cari and started to circle her.

"If you come near me, I'll call my friends" Cari shouted out in a trembling voice.

"And where are your friends?" asked the wolf.

"They're up the hill," replied Cari, waving the staff in front of herself.

The wolf stopped in his tracks and stared at Cari waving the staff.

"That staff looks very familiar," the wolf said, staring at it.

"It belongs to the curator," Cari replied. "He gave it to me to travel with my friends."

"Looks like there's something missing from its tip," the wolf suggested in his menacing tone.

"There is," replied Cari. "Someone stole the head and is taking it to a table or something, to open his world up, I don't really understand." Cari was so scared by now she stated to cry. "I wish my Zeff was here."

She had no idea why she had called her pet and protector Sam by his god name, but on hearing this, the wolf quickly backed away.

"You said Zeff, do you know Zeff?" asked the wolf.

"I know my Sam is a wolf god called Zeff, and that he has two brothers, and one sister. Two of his brothers are with him chasing after the head from this staff, and if you hurt me, they will come for you, and you will be very sorry."

"Two brothers, you say, and both of them are with him. What about their sister?" asked the wolf.

"I don't know," replied Cari. "They said she liked to be alone."

"You said Zeff," continued the menacing wolf, still glaring at Cari. "Do the names Marrok and Amoux mean anything to you?" The wolf asked in its menacing tone.

"They are my Sam's brothers," Cari replied. "If you hurt me, they will come and get you."

"What is your name, human?" the wolf asked, staring with her fiery eyes.

"My name is Cari and I wish my Sam was here."

"You fear me because of my tone and appearances don't you, Cari? My name is Amarok. I am their sister. You must trust me, and I really mean you no harm. Zeff, Marrok and Amoux are my brothers and I fear Zeff more than anything. He is my eldest brother and I would never do anything to make him angry. You fear the darkness because you can't see without light, I live in the dark because of my appearance, not because I am bad. My brothers made stories up about me when we were growing up and the stories stuck to my name. Do you know who has the head from your staff?"

"The curator said something about him being, half-human, half-wolf."

"Did he mention the name Anubis?"

"Yes, that's it," Cari replied feeling less afraid of the wolf now.

"You need to trust me Cari, as you would trust Zeff. Climb onto my back and hold on really tight to my neck. I will take you to the hilltop. I know what Anubis plans to do, and he mustn't be allowed to succeed."

Cari climbed onto the back of the wolf, Amarok, placing the staff firmly under her arm so as not to drop it, and held on very tight with her arms around her neck.

Then Amarok started to run up the hill with Cari holding on so very tight in fear of falling off.

THE WOLF GOD AMAROK

Cari could feel the wind blowing in her face so knew they must be travelling really fast, even though it was too dark for her to see if they were. The ride was smooth, it really felt like they were flying,

But that couldn't be right, Cari thought to herself, dogs and wolves can't fly. But then again, she thought, nothing seams normal here anyway. They seemed to be travelling for a very long time. As they approached the top of the hill, Cari could see the sun just starting to rise again on the horizon. Either I fell asleep while travelling, or the nights are very short here, she thought to herself.

As they approached the summit she could hear and feel that there must be a battle going on. The ground was shaking, the wind was howling, and she could hear the sounds of birds which really frightened her.

Amarok, Cari's new wolf friend, started slowing down, she stopped short of the battleground, at a distance where she knew Cari would be safe.

"You better get off now, Cari, stay here out of harm's way."

She could see Sam pounding the floor making the ground shake, and hear Fluff howling, making the wind howl back with as much strength as it could. Max was talking to the birds who were swooping down, kicking the staff's head just out of reach of Anubis, just as he was about to grab hold of it.

The menacing shadows had gained an almost solid form now, and were making the fight very difficult for Sam, Max and Fluff; all three of them were under attack, and struggling just to keep the head of the staff out of arm's reach from Anubis. There seemed to be no hope in sight of them stopping Anubis from gaining power. All three were tiring from their ordeal, and it was looking as though their efforts would be in vain, and all would be lost, as they wouldn't be able to complete their task without the curator's staff, which Cari had, and they had no idea how long it would take her to get to them.

Cari's new wolf friend, Amarok, slowly walked into the arena where all this was happening.

"Anubis," she shouted.

This startled everyone, and for a few seconds their concentration was interrupted. Sam stopped pounding the ground so the quaking stopped, Fluff stopped howling and the wind dropped, and Max stopped talking to the birds, so they thought their work was done and flew away.

"Anubis," shouted the wolf, Amarok. "You need to go back from where you came. You don't belong here, you are interfering with time."

Sam, Max and Fluff all turned and looked at each other in amazement; none of them expected their sister, Amarok, to show herself.

But this interference with the brothers' concentration enabled Anubis to grab the head of the curator's staff. He now had it in his hand and was only a short distance from the Tizoc Stone.

Sam Max and Fluff composed themselves and continued their efforts to try and stop Anubis from succeeding with his determination of taking control of time.

The menacing forms which Anubis had summoned to aid him, had disappeared on seeing Amarok.

Anubis raised his staff and thrust it to the ground to summon them once more.

"Do you actually think those demons will do your bidding while I am present?" Amarok shouted in a dominating growling tone.

Sam was extremely surprised. His little sister's reputation, although not really correct, had even been passed down and recognised in the underworld. The spirit demons were more afraid of Amarok than they were of Anubis.

Sam was tiring, and his pounding on the ground was having less and less effect. Anubis steadied himself on his legs and lifted the wolf head of the staff, ready to offer it to his own staff.

Max and Fluff were tiring too, as the battle to stop Anubis getting to the stone of Tizoc had been going on all night, and didn't seem to have any positive outcome, as Cari had the curator's staff which was needed to end it all.

Amarok ran forward and leapt between Anubis and the Tizoc Stone blocking his way.

Sam, Max and Fluff ran forward to attack Anubis, but with one sweep of his staff Anubis knocked them back. They were completely exhausted from their night's ordeal.

Amarok stood her ground, not daring to move, or give in, even though she was now alone in the fight.

"Let me past, Amarok, and I'll let you reign beside me. We will share the power of time together." Anubis moved toward Amarok, raised his staff in his right hand and raised the head for the staff in his left hand, ready to place them together.

Cari had been watching from where her wolf friend, Amarok, had left her, safe from harm's way.

She saw Sam, Max and Fluff charge at Anubis and watched as Anubis used his staff to swipe them away as if it were no effort at all. She saw her Sam lying on the ground not able to move. This was the one thing that burned her with anger, she had no fear of anything now.

All she cared about was her Sam, and seeing him lying there motionless gave her the courage to race forward and do whatever she could to try and get her Sam back again to the way he was. She had no care for her own safety for the first time in her life; all that she cared about was her Sam.

Cari held the curator's staff tight in both hands and ran towards Anubis.

Amarok looked past Anubis and saw her running towards them; she wondered what Cari thought she was doing. She had told her to stay away, a human was no match for this evil god. Then Amarok saw that Cari had the curator's staff held out in front of her as she was running toward them. What was she hoping to achieve? Amarok thought to herself.

Amarok kept Anubis looking at her by asking, "What are you offering to me?"

Anubis felt confident that he was in total control now, and Amarok could be persuaded to join him.

Cari ran towards them both. Her thoughts were to use the staff to knock the staff head from the hand of Anubis.

What she didn't expect was that, when the curator's staff came in contact with the head it would once again attach itself firmly.

Cari hit the wolf head hard with the staff of the curator. The head of the staff instantly attached itself back on the curator's staff, Anubis turned around swiftly in anger, narrowly missing Cari with the full force of his staff.

This gave Amarok a chance to show her true loyalty to her brothers, and her new human friend.

Amarok swiftly placed herself between Anubis and Cari.

Amarok shouted to Cari, "Go to Zeff, touch him with the staff."

Cari ran towards her Sam lying motionless on the ground. Tears were rolling down her face, as she thought her Sam was dead.

She did as her new wolf friend had told her; she touched her Sam with the staff of the curator.

A bright light came from the head on the tip of the staff and completely engulfed Sam lying there. The light from the curator's staff slowly faded and Cari looked at Sam. His eyes opened and he quickly got to his feet. "Do the same to my brothers, quickly," said Sam.

Amarok was now in battle with Anubis, Amarok being beaten with Anubis's staff every time she charged at him hoping to sink her teeth into him.

With every contact Amarok had with the staff, it drained more and more of her strength.

With a final blow from the staff of Anubis, Amarok fell to the ground.

Anubis now turned to Cari "Give me that staff," he shouted.

Cari ran to Sam's brothers also lying motionless. She did as Sam had asked and the same thing happened, a bright light from the stone at the tip of the staff engulfed them in turn and they jumped to their feet as if recharged with full strength.

Sam started to pound the ground as before and Anubis became unsteady on his feet.

Cari fell to the ground too, unable to stand with the ground shaking so violently. *"Give me that staff,"* shouted Anubis as he slowly crawled towards Cari.

Fluff howled once more. The wind gained strength with more force than before and stopped Anubis in his tracks. Anubis raised his staff and thrust it to the ground as he did before.

With Amarok looking lifeless, the demons returned and began charging at Sam, Max and Fluff.

"The curator's staff," shouted Sam. "It needs to be placed on the Stone of Tizoc."

Max looked at Cari, unable to move due to the ground shaking. She had the curator's staff, tightly in her grip.

"Cari" shouted Max, "close your eyes and do not open them until I tell you. You must keep tight hold of the staff, hold it with both hands above your head, and keep your eyes tightly shut. No matter what you feel, do not open your eyes until I say."

Cari was frightened. What was going to happen?

RESTORATION

Cari was frightened but did as she was told by Max. She held the staff very tightly above her head and closed her eyes.

Cari heard Max Give out a long "woooooof."

She knew Max could control the birds and was very scared of what she couldn't see, but was even more afraid of what she might see.

Cari felt something grasp the staff. She was very tempted to open her eyes but Max shouted again, "Keep your eyes tightly closed Cari, don't open them until I say."

Cari felt herself being lifted from the ground; something was pulling her up. "Must keep my eyes closed, must keep my eyes closed," she kept saying to herself.

Then she felt the ground beneath her feet again. Max shouted, "Cari, it's okay now, you can open your eyes."

Cari opened her eyes to see two giant eagles flying away; they had lifted her and taken her to stand beside the Tizoc Stone.

Sam, Max and Fluff all shouted together, *"Touch the stone with the staff."*

Cari did as she was told, still staring at the eagles now flying into the distance.

She touched the Tizoc Stone with the staff which was now complete with its head firmly attached again.

There was a blinding light, much brighter than when she touched Sam and his brothers with it.

The bright light faded and started to change into multiple colours, the same, coloured lights she had seen in the cave when the curator was talking to them.

Sam, Max, Fluff and their sister wolf now stood in silence looking at Anubis. Anubis stood upright again, surrounded by his demons, and ordered them to attack.

Cari felt someone, or something, had taken hold of the staff she was holding. "I'll take it now, Cari," said a soft quiet voice. It was a voice she had heard before, the voice of the curator.

The staff moved into the glowing lights. The demons, seeing this, sank back down into the cracks in the ground from where they came.

The curator spoke. "You, Anubis have failed. I have my staff back in my possession, you will return to your world, never to return here ever again."

The curator's staff started to spin. It gathered speed and made a wailing sound. The demons which had retreated down the cracks in the earth were returning now under the control of the curator.

The demons took hold of Anubis and started to pull him towards the largest of the cracks *"You won't keep me away,"* shouted Anubis. *"I will return again, I will have the wolf head on my staff one day, just wait and see."* With his last words the demons dragged him down, back to the underworld where he belonged, and the cracks in the ground slowly sealed themselves.

THE RETURN HOME

The curator had control once again, Cari watched as the light from where the voice came, slowly turned into a mist. She stared into the mist, trying to see what the creator actually looked like. Maybe it's another wolf she thought to herself.

The mist slowly faded and to Cari's amazement there stood an old man. His hair was very long and pure white, just like her Sam's fur. He wore a long robe which she thought looked like the robe a wizard would wear.

"Your work is done now," said the curator. "It is time for me to repair the crack in time and for you all to return home. But first, we shall return to my cave to rest and eat."

Cari thought about the long journey, how long it had taken to get where they were now, that wasn't something she was looking forward to.

Sam, his two brothers, and their sister came together, and sat in front of the curator.

"Now that I have my powers back, we can return to my cave safely. I'm getting a little bit old for wandering around on hills, but I will accompany you on the journey."

Amarok, with fire and anger in her eyes, stood and faced the curator. "Why did you not summon me in this quest to help my brothers?" she shouted.

The curator replied in a very soft and calming voice. "I did summon you as best as I could, with what little powers I had left. You did find Cari and my staff, didn't you?"

"Well, that was not by chance. I knew my time was running short, and Cari might have been left behind while your brothers ran ahead. I knew once you saw my staff you would help Cari and join your brothers in the fight."

Amarok sat down again next to her brothers. "I thought you had forgotten me. I don't really like being alone, it's just that I don't like scaring anyone with the way I look. That's why I only come out at night. I can't be seen in the dark with being as black as the night."

Cari walked over to Amarok and put her arm around her, "I was afraid of you at first, but now I know that you are really a kind, and good-hearted wolf god, just like your brothers, Sam, Max, and Fluff are."

They all started to descend the hill. Sam had repaired the pathway he had made on the ascent to make it easier for Cari and the curator to walk along.

Sam, Max and Fluff walked together. They had lots to talk about with not seeing each other for such a long time. They talked about their lives living amongst humans. Cari walked with the curator and Amarok, but felt a little awkward not knowing what to say to start a conversation, and Amarok felt a little left out with her brothers not inviting her to join them.

Cari was starting to feel tired. Amarok saw this and pushed her head under Cari's arm. "Cari?" said Amarok, "you do look so very tired. Would you like to ride on my back again?'

The curator smiled and was happy to hear this. Amarok wasn't at all like her reputation of being a devil dog. She was kind and gentle. Cari nodded her head and climbed onto Amarok's back, holding on tightly by putting her arms around her neck. Amarok was happy with this too. She had never felt the touch of a human before this night, it felt so good to her. She felt for the first time in her life that someone could love her, even if she did look fierce. This was something the curator was looking for in Amarok, and all the proof he needed to make a decision that would change Amarok's life forever.

They finally arrived at the foot of the hill and the entrance to the curators cave.

"Let us all go in," said the curator. "I have a celebration feast set out in the great hall, and I have an announcement to make."

The curator opened the door to the cave and they all entered walking along the passage which led to the great hall. "Sit, eat and drink," said the curator. They all did this without saying a word. Cari sat between Sam and Amarok and now and then would offer food to each of them in turn.

The curator stood up and banged his staff on the table to get everyone's attention.

"You will all be returning to your own place in time soon, but first I have an announcement to make. Amarok, come here and stand in front of me."

Amarok left the table and walked toward the curator. She wondered what she had done wrong. She really thought that the curator was going to discipline her and tell her off for something she had done.

"Amarok," said the curator, "you tonight have shown to me that you are not really the devil wolf dog you are thought to be. You have never had contact with a human until tonight, but you showed kindness. Because you have never had a human family, you have never had a name that a human could call you by. I being the curator, the keeper of time, do now give you a name that will be used by your human family, that will soon find you. You will care and look after them just as you have cared for Cari and your brothers. The name that I give you will still be recognised in the underworld, and you will keep evil under control with fear of this name. The name that I give you is Kira."

The curator touched Amarok with his staff and everyone stood up. Cari clapped her hands and cheered while Sam, Max and Fluff howled, and ran toward their sister to show how happy they were.

"Kira," Amarok said. "I have a name for a human to call me, when will a human choose me?" asked Amarok.

"Somewhere in time," replied the Curator, "in time."

The wolves knew this could mean anything from, she already has a family but in a different time from where she has been living, to maybe she will find a family in the future, or the past.

The curator controlled time, and kept it in time, with the time it was meant to be, in time.

The curator spoke again. "Cari, please come forward."

Cari walked to stand in front of the curator. "I want you to do something for me. I would like you to take this staff with you when you return with Zeff to your own time. It will be safer with you, in human time. Only I will know where to find it if it is needed again, but first I will repair the window in time, and will try to make it stronger than before."

THE CURATOR

Cari thought to herself, maybe he should try double glazing.

Max, Fluff and the newly named Kira said their goodbyes to Sam and Cari, and made their way to the places where they found themselves when the curator had first called them.

Cari was feeling and looking very tired. The curator spoke to her and Sam. "You both can rest on the straw bedding, while I complete my work by sending Max and Fluff to their human times and homes. Kira will go back to the forest and fall asleep, but will wake up in the human world and find a family to live with and protect."

Cari lay down with Sam next to her. She put her arm around him, feeling safe being close to him.

The curator set about his tasks of repairing the crack in time and returning Sam's brothers to their point in human time.

Cari could hear him mumbling, and hear faint cracking sounds. She was very comfortable laying on the straw and started to drift off to sleep.

The mumbling voice started to change, and as the cracking sounds faded away, she heard her name being called. "Cari, Cari, come on, sleepy, dinner is ready."

Cari opened her eyes. She was back home and her mum was calling her in for dinner. She sat up and looked all around. Sam was still lying down but opened his eyes and looked at Cari. "Come on," Mum called. "Your dinner's getting cold."

Cari could still remember everything that had happened. Was it real or was I dreaming, she thought to herself. She walked into the kitchen followed by Sam. "Sorry, Mum," she said, "but I don't really feel hungry. I think I'll just go upstairs to bed for a while."

"Okay," Mum replied, "you can eat later, if you feel like it."

Cari still felt confused. I really must have been dreaming, she thought to herself, but I don't feel hungry after eating all the food in my dream, that's really strange.

Cari walked into the living room and headed towards the stairs to go to her bedroom.

Sam stopped her by grabbing her hand. "What's up, Sam, what do you want?"

Sam turned her around, let go of her hand, and walked to the corner of the living room. Cari looked to where Sam had walked and saw a stick, a tall walking stick with a dog's head attached to the top.

"*Mum*," Cari shouted, "where did this dog headed walking stick come from?"

Cari's mum walked into the living room. "Oh, I don't know, maybe it's something your dad brought home with him."

Cari thought to herself, that looks just like the stick I was given to look after.

Cari turned and started to climb the stairs, still thinking how she could dream about a stick and then see it in her home.

Sam followed her as he always did and sat at the foot of the stairs, watching Cari, making sure she was safe.

Cari was halfway up the stairs, when heard a quiet voice behind her. "Goodnight, Cari," the voice said.

She stopped and turned around to see Sam smiling and looking at her from the foot of the stairs. No, she thought, it couldn't be. She stared at Sam and said quietly, so her mum couldn't hear, "Sam, did you just say something?"

Sam winked with one eye, stood up and walked back into the living room.

THE HOLIDAY

Cari woke up from a very deep sleep. She could hear Mum and Dad downstairs talking.

This was the day they were going away for a holiday. She was still slightly confused about the previous day's events, and couldn't decide if what had happened was real, or herself just dreaming.

"Come on, sleepy, it's time to get ready for our holiday." Her mum was calling her to get ready.

Dad was busy loading the car with cases, and things they were going to need while they were away from home.

"I think that's everything in the car now," Dad said. "We just need to get ready ourselves, and then, we're off.

Cari still had no idea where they were going, but that didn't matter, as long as it was somewhere by the sea.

Cari got out of bed, got herself ready for holiday and walked down the stairs, remembering that she thought that she had heard Sam say goodnight to her, when she was going up the stairs to bed.

I must have been really tired to imagine that, she thought to herself.

Cari walked into the living room and her eyes instantly looked into the corner of the room. The stick was still there. Well, I didn't imagine seeing that, she thought.

"Come on," said Dad. "We need to make tracks, we've a long way to go, to get to the holiday cottage."

They all went out to the car, Cari and Sam being the first, they always sat together on the back seat. They fastened themselves in the car with the seatbelts. Sam had a special seatbelt made just for dogs. He didn't really like having put on, but even he knew it must be necessary if Cari had to wear one.

"I'll just do one more check to make sure we have everything we need," said Cari's dad, "and then, we'll get on our way."

For some reason, Cari thought about the staff lying against the wall, in the corner of the living room.

"Dad," shouted Cari, can we take the long walking stick with us that's in the living room?"

"Okay, I'll bring it once I've checked the house," Cari's dad shouted back.

Cari's dad set their destination on the satnav in the car and they started on their journey, for their holiday.

"Dad," asked Cari, "where did you get this dog's head stick from?"

"Well," said Cari's dad, "that's a very strange thing. I was walking Sam early yesterday morning, as usual, around the park before I go to work, when we saw a very strange old man. He was just standing by the edge of the park. We don't usually see anyone that early in the morning. He looked like he was waiting for someone. Sam seemed to think he was okay. He ran up to him and made friends straight away. So I thought, if Sam thinks he's okay, then he must be. The man started asking me about Sam. He was very interested in him. He said that he had four dogs of his own, but they weren't with him any more, I think he meant that they had died.

"Anyway, he had that staff in his hand and asked me to hold it for him while he fastened his shoe lace. I think Sam saw something, he started barking and ran across the field. I turned away from the old man, only for a few seconds to call Sam back, and, when I turned back he had gone. I had that very unusual stick in my hand and the old man had just disappeared, he just seemed to vanish. I looked all around to see where he had gone, but there wasn't any sign of him anywhere, so we brought the stick home with us. I'm sure it looked different to how it does now, or maybe it was me just not looking at it properly."

Their journey to the holiday cottage took most of the day.

Sam slept next to Cari, now and then opening one eye to check everything was okay, he wasn't bothered about travelling so long as he was together with his family.

Cari got bored just looking out of the car window. There wasn't much really to see, only cars, trucks and road direction signs, and now and then fields with cows grassing.

"Are we nearly there yet?" asked Cari.

"Almost" replied her dad, "we should be there very soon, not far to go now."

They eventually arrived at the cottage Dad had rented for their holiday.

The cottage was just a short walk away from the sea.

"We'll unpack the car later," said Cari's dad. "Let us all have a walk to see the sea before it starts to get dark."

Sam thought that was a very good idea. He hadn't had chance to have a decent walk all day. He wagged his tail in excitement, not about going to the sea, because he really didn't like getting wet, but because he loved a nice walk.

Cari grabbed the staff. "Dad, can I take this with me?"

"Okay, it might be helpful, some pathways can be vey steep around here."

They arrived at a point looking down to the sea from a hilltop. The sea looked very calm and inviting.

"Can we go down to the beach?' asked Cari.

"Yes, why not," came the reply from her dad.

They walked down a very steep path which led to the beach.

The sound and smell of the sea, in the warm sea breeze, made the walk feel very exciting.

Cari looked down towards the beach from the path they were taking.

"Hey look," she shouted. "There's a cave."

"Can we go inside to explore?"

"Maybe, we will see," came the reply from Cari's dad.

They arrived on the shoreline and looked out to sea. The sea breeze was very relaxing.

"Hey, look Cari, there's a dog the same as Sam in the sea. You wouldn't catch Sam doing that, would you?"

Cari laughed. "No, you wouldn't," she replied. "He really hates getting wet."

Sam looked very happy to see that he had someone to play with on the beach.

Sam ran towards the dog from the sea and they both ran around together in a very playful mood.

"I wonder where its owner is?" said Caris dad. "It's very strange to see a Samoyed all alone," he continued.

"Maybe he lives local and just walks himself, some dogs do that."

Sam and his new friend ran towards the cave.

"Dad, can I go with Sam to see the cave?"

"Okay. But be very careful, and don't go climbing on the rocks, they can be very slippery."

"Okay, Dad, I'll be careful, I've got the staff to help me." Cari followed Sam and his new friend. They had run ahead and both entered the cave. Cari took a few minutes to catch them up and get to the cave entrance.

The cave was dark inside and it took a minute for Cari's eyes to adjust to the lack of light.

"Sam," Cari called, "where are you?"

"We are here, keep walking towards my voice, the ground is level so you will not fall."

Cari recognised the voice. It was Sam speaking again.

"You can speak," said Cari. "I thought everything yesterday was just a dream."

She saw Sam and his new friend sitting together waiting for her to arrive.

She stood looking at them both, then suddenly she remembered what Sam had told her, he had a brother who looked like a Samoyed in the human world.

She looked closer at Sam's new friend. "Fluff, it's you, isn't it? "I remember, you are the spirit of water, that's where you came from, you came out of the sea, didn't you?"

Sam's new friend looked at Sam and then at Cari.

"Yes, Cari, I am Fluff. Something must have happened on your return home from the curators cave. You are not supposed to remember what had happened, it was just meant for you to believe it was a dream that you had."

Sam stood up. "I knew there was something wrong. Cari didn't eat her dinner last night after that feast we all had, she just went straight to bed. She should have still felt hungry, believing it was all a dream."

"I see you have brought the staff with you," Fluff said. "If you remember what Sam told you, I am also the spirit of memory. I will try and wipe clear all the thoughts in your head of the events that happened to us all yesterday."

"Is it going to hurt?" asked Cari in a shaky voice.

"No," said Fluff, "it won't hurt, you won't feel a thing. We would never hurt you. You might feel a bit light headed, and as the sun sets, all should return to as it should be."

Fluff continued to talk to Cari. "I would like you to hold the staff in front of yourself, and stare at the head of the staff, concentrate on the head on the staff, empty your mind of everything else, all you see is the staff, all you hear is the sound of my voice."

Cari did as she was told. She held the staff in both hands and stared at the dog's head sitting on the head of the staff.

She heard Fluff say something to Sam in dog language, followed by a very soft sounding whine it was like Fluff was singing, the sound was quite soothing and relaxing.

She continued to stay focused on the head of the staff, staring at the dog's head attached to it.

She noticed the eyes in the head of the staff starting to glow. The glowing eyes got brighter. Cari's eyes were firmly attached to it, staring deeply into the eyes of the dog's head, on the staff.

The glow faded, and it seemed to Cari as if nothing had really happened other than Sam and Fluff having a sing together, and a strange feeling that the dog's head on the staff had come alive and was staring back at her.

Cari could hear her dad calling "Cari, come on, it's time we went back to the cottage."

Cari turned to leave the cave. "Come on, Sam, it's time to go."

They both ran back to the beach where Cari's dad was waiting.

"Did you see anything interesting?" asked her dad.

"Not really, just a very damp and dark empty cave."

They all started to walk up the steep path back to their holiday cottage.

Cari's dad wondered to himself where the other Samoyed had gone. He never saw it come out of the cave with Cari and Sam.

They arrived back at the holiday cottage. Cari's dad unpacked the car while her mum started to prepare something for their dinner.

Cari said, "I'm going to sit outside with Sam for a while, call me when dinner is ready."

She took a chair outside and sat on it holding the staff and examining it very closely. Sam sat next to her.

The sun was starting to go down. It looked like it was falling into the sea. The sky was changing colour as the sun slowly dropped. The sky was now a fiery red over the sea and Cari thought it looked very beautiful.

She looked into the eyes of the dog's head that was sitting on top of the staff, the eyes seemed to glow as the sun was going down.

Cari and Sam watched the sun slowly starting to disappear. She put her arm around Sam's neck.

"I wonder where that Samoyed went that you were playing with?"

Sam looked at her, smiled and said nothing.